Enid Blyton's
RUMBLE AND CHUFF
and other stories from the playroom

Illustrated by Jenny Norton

HAMLYN

Contents

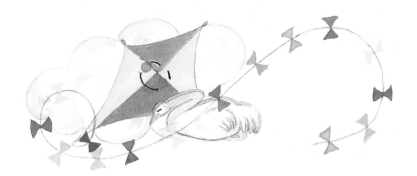

Rumble and Chuff

 There was once a fine wooden engine. It was painted mostly red and yellow, and it had three trucks behind it, one red, one blue, and one green.

It was big enough to carry most of the dolls in the playroom, and teddy bear and the stripy cat. It belonged to John and Lucy, and always stood in its own corner, by the window.

The two children did not look after their toys very well, not even the fine wooden engine. The paint was soon scratched and dented, and the funnel came loose. One of the trucks was trodden on and all the wheels came off.

The engine was very worried. "Soon I shall be no use," it said to the cat. "I don't like these children. I wish I could run away."

9

"But who would drive you?" said the cat. "You couldn't go puffing off by yourself. Stay with us—perhaps John and Lucy will learn to be more careful."

They didn't learn. Two days later the engine had only one truck! John had dropped the second one out of the window, and it had smashed to bits on the ground below. The engine was very sad—only one truck left! Soon it wouldn't be a train at all!

Now, when the truck fell out of the window, it almost hit a toy clown who was sitting in the sun. John had left him out in the garden a few weeks before and now he lived there. He was most astonished to see a blue truck come hurtling down and smash to pieces.

"Oh, dear!" he said. "A truck! A beautiful truck, all smashed to bits. I wonder where the engine is? I hope that won't come flying out of the window too! I'll go and see if it's all right. I *am* so fond of trains!"

Well, the clown climbed up the ivy on the wall and jumped down into the nursery—and the first thing he saw was the engine near by, looking most unhappy.

"Hallo!" said the clown. "Was that your truck that fell out of the window? What happened?"

"It's those children," said the engine, speaking in its funny rumbling voice. "I wish I could run away! I shan't be a train much longer if I stay here. But there's nobody to drive me!"

"Do you want someone to drive you?" cried the clown. "Well, what about *me*? My name's Chuff— Mr Chuff—and if that isn't a good name for the driver of an engine I'd like to know a better one! Let *me* drive you! We'll have a fine time together. What's your name?"

"Rumble," said the engine in delight. "Oh, do, *do* be my driver. We'll go about together and have lots of fine adventures! Goodbye, Cat; goodbye, Dolls; goodbye, Teddy—I'm off with my one truck, and Mr Chuff to drive me!"

Well, what do you think of that? Mr Chuff got into the cab of the engine, and took a whistle from his pocket. He always kept one there just in *case* he ever had a chance to drive a train!

Wheeeeee. He whistled loudly, and Rumble the engine ran happily over the floor and out of the door, pulling the one red truck behind. Everyone waved goodbye.

"We're off!" said Chuff. "All by ourselves. We'll go anywhere we like, and give people rides, and have the best adventures in the world."

The wooden engine rumbled down the path, with Mr Chuff in the little cab holding on to the steering wheel. They were both very excited.

"Where shall we go?" said Chuff. "Let's puff along to the woods, Rumble, and run down the rabbits' paths. It will be shady and cool there. We can get out of the sun on this hot summer's day!"

So they took a little path that ran in and out of the trees, and didn't the rabbits jump out of the way when they saw the little train coming along the path at top speed!

When they came to the heart of the wood Mr Chuff stopped the engine. "Listen!" he said. "Stay quiet a minute! Can you hear something?"

They both listened. The engine gave a little puff. "Yes! It sounds like someone crying. Let's find out who it is."

Chuff started the engine again, and they set off down another path. The noise was louder—and then, when the little engine ran around a big oak-tree, what did Mr Chuff see but a small girl sitting on the grass crying! He jumped out at once.

"What's the matter?" he said. "Can we help you? Have you fallen down? Have you lost something?"

"No," said the little girl. "At least—I've lost myself. I don't know my way home—and I'm f-f-f-frightened!"

The engine gave an excited rumble. "I'll take her! I'll take her!"

"But you're too small," said Chuff to Rumble. "Still, we can soon do something about that! Wait now—what's the spell to make small things big? Yes—I remember it!"

He took a little blue
duster from his pocket, and
rubbed the engine and the
truck from top to bottom.
These are the magic words
he said:

"Filly-tar-roony,
    Abra-carray,
Listen to all
    The words that I say.
Grow, little engine,
    Grow—grow—GROW.
Filly-tar-roony,
    Abra-car-RO!"

And just as he said the
last word, the engine began
to grow, and so did the
truck. My word, it did look
fine! It was quite big

enough now to take the little girl easily in the truck. She climbed in at once, smiling all over her face.

"Hey—*I'm* too small now!" said Mr Chuff, in dismay. "Don't go without me. I'll polish myself with my magic duster and say the words again."

So he did—and he grew too, till he was just the right size for the engine. He got into the cab and blew his whistle. *Wheeeeeeeeee.*

And off they went through the wood, taking the little girl safely home. When they got a little way, she saw a path she knew. But she wouldn't get out of the truck. Oh, no—she wanted to go all the way home in this lovely wooden truck!

"Here we are!" she said, at last, and she got out of the truck. "Come into my garden. There's a little summerhouse there, and we could have tea together without anyone knowing. I do so like you, Rumble and Chuff!"

And so, if anyone had peeped into that little house, they would have seen the little girl, Mr Chuff and Rumble the engine all together, enjoying themselves very much.

Mr Chuff ate buns and biscuits. Rumble had lemonade poured down his funnel, and he said it was delicious.

After tea, Rumble and Chuff said goodbye to the little girl and they set off to look for another adventure.

"Here we go," said Mr Chuff. "Rumble— rumble—chuff, chuff, chuff."

The Grand Doll

There was once a very grand doll, dressed just like a king. He had a golden crown on his head, and a red cloak that flowed out round him.

He was very grand indeed, and he thought a lot of himself. He sat in the toyshop and spoke to the other toys.

"I shall soon be bought and taken to a lovely home. I shall be king of all the toys there. I shall rule them, and make them bow down to me."

So, when he was bought, and taken to the fine playroom full of toys, he was pleased. He looked round at the dolls and animals, and spoke in a high and mighty voice.

"Good evening! I am a king-doll. Do you see my crown? I shall rule over you and be your king."

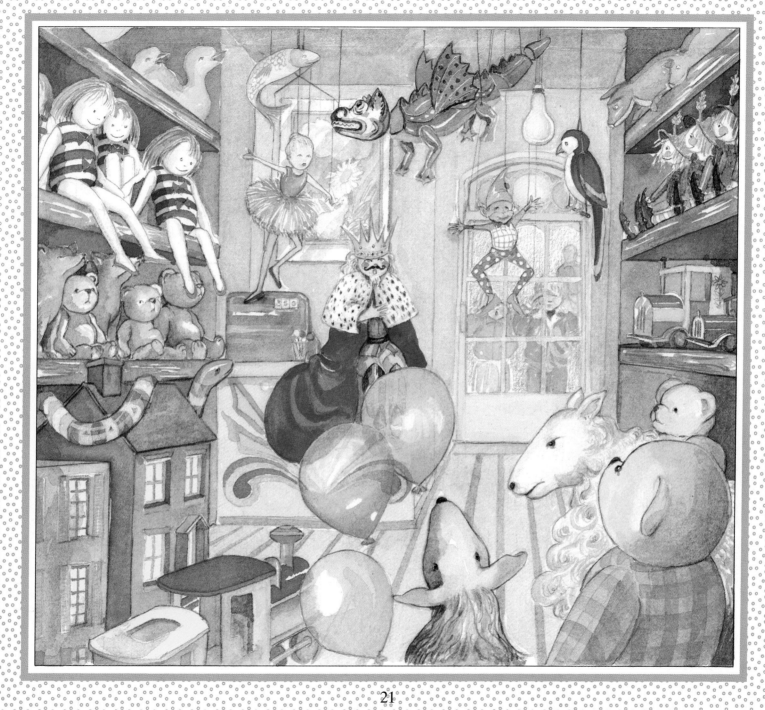

Nobody said anything. The clockwork mouse gave a little giggle, and the king-doll glared at him.

"Did you all hear what I said? I am your king, and you are lucky to have me."

"Well, we don't want you," said the sailor-doll. "We have a queen, and we don't want a king."

"Where's your queen?" said the king-doll, looking all round for a doll that wore a crown and looked as grand as he did. But he didn't see one.

"This is our queen," said the sailor-doll, and he took the arm of a dear little doll, with a kind face, a plain red dress, and two golden plaits. She smiled, and her eyes looked kind.

"What a funny sort of queen to have!" said the king-doll, and he laughed unkindly. "Not at all pretty—dressed in an old red dress— not even a crown on her head! And she looks rather stupid too."

"Don't talk of our queen like that!" squeaked the clockwork mouse, crossly. "I shall bite you if you do."

"No, no," said the queen-doll. "You musn't speak like that, Mouse. You know I have never wanted to be a queen. You must have this fine doll for your king—he looks very grand."

"Well—he can be king as well, and we'll see how he gets on," said the clown. The king-doll was pleased. He set his crown quite straight, and looked round for a throne.

23

He chose a pretty chair and made the sailor-doll fetch a cushion or two out of the dolls' house for him to sit on.

"Now you shall all practise your bows," he said. "People have to bow to kings. And you must each think of a nice present to give me."

But nobody came to bow, and nobody gave him a present. Instead they went to the queen-doll, who was sewing, and she told them a story.

Nobody paid much attention to the grand king-doll. Nobody seemed even to want to talk to him, or hear his tales of the toyshop and all he did there. He was so cross because the clockwork mouse giggled at him that he smacked him hard, and the little mouse went crying to the queen-doll.

She gave him a blue ribbon to tie round his neck, so he soon stopped crying.

The king-doll looked across at the little queen-doll, with her golden plaits.

"She's always busy at something," he thought crossly. "Kings and queens oughtn't to work hard, as she does. Whatever does she do all the time?"

Sometimes she mended the clown's coat, which was always getting torn. Once she sewed up a hole in a small teddy bear. He had caught himself on a nail, and his stuffing was leaking out. It frightened him, so the queen-doll sewed up the hole and made him all right again.

The queen-doll settled quarrels too. Sometimes the teddy bear fought the clown, and then the queen-doll stopped them, and made them say they were sorry. She took the clockwork mouse on her

26

knee and was kind to him when somebody
trod on his tail, which very often happened.

"Good gracious, she's nothing more than a silly
little mother to all the toys!" said the king-doll to
himself in great disgust. "Wasting her time like
that! Why doesn't she make the toys work for her,
and sew her a beautiful dress and cloak instead of
that old red dress? Why doesn't she make them say
'Your Majesty' and bow to her when they speak?"

When a week had gone
by the king-doll called
a meeting of the toys,
and he spoke to them in his
grand, high-and-mighty voice.
"Toys! I have watched you
for a week, and I want to tell
you that your queen-doll is not
a queen at all. She just acts like a
silly little mother, fussing over you, and
working hard instead of making you fuss
over her and work for her. It's all wrong. She
doesn't know how to be a queen. But I know
how to be a king! So why don't you choose
me, and have a king instead of a queen.
I'd be a king you could be proud of."

"Pooh!" said the clown, rudely. "We'd never be proud of you! You're dreadful! You're vain and selfish and lazy!"

"We want someone to love and someone who loves us," squeaked the clockwork mouse. "That's the best sort of ruler to have—somebody like ourselves, but kinder and wiser, who understands us, and loves us and wants us to be happy. You would be a bad king!"

"Be quiet!" said the king-doll, crossly.

"I don't really want to be queen," said the little doll with golden plaits, smiling at the king-doll. "I don't feel a queen. You can be king if you want to, but let me still love the toys and look after them."

The king-doll suddenly felt ashamed of himself. He knew the queen-doll was better and wiser and kinder than he was. He knew that he was vain and lazy and selfish, just as the clown had said. He loved the little queen-doll and he wanted her to love him too, just as she loved the other toys. He realized what he should do.

He took off his golden crown and set it on the little doll's golden head. He took off his red cloak and put it gently round her shoulders.

"There!" he said. "Now you are a real queen. "My queen, as well. I should never make as good a king as you are a queen. I will be an ordinary doll, and love you as the others do. I can see that you are queen of all our hearts, as well as queen of the playroom!"

Well, wasn't that nice of him? All the toys cheered loudly, and the little queen-doll went red with delight. To think she had a crown and a cloak! Dear, dear, whatever would happen next?

The king-doll kept his word. He was just an ordinary doll, and he loved the little queen, and did everything he could for her. And one day I think the toys will really make him their king—but he will have earned his crown and cloak then, and that is the best way for him to get them, isn't it?

The Quiet Kite

When the kite came to live in the playroom the other toys couldn't understand it at all.

"It's not a doll," said the red-haired doll.

"It's not a bear," said the teddy.

"It's not an engine," said the train.

"It's a silly sort of toy," said the rocking horse, looking into the toy cupboard, where the kite lay quiet and still. "It has no legs, so it can't run about with us. It can't even roll, like the balls!"

"It has a tail, but doesn't wag it," said the pink dog, who was very proud of his tail because it wagged to and fro when he was wound up.

Everyone looked at the kite's long tail. It was made of screwed-up bits of paper tied to a string.

The kite suddenly spoke, in a kind of windy, wheezy voice. "I daren't move my tail in case it gets tangled up," it said. "It takes such a time to untangle it, you know."

"Oh, the kite can talk!" cried the red-haired doll. "Do come out and play, Kite."

"No, thank you," said the kite. "As the rocking horse said, I have no legs, so I can't walk. I prefer to stay here quietly."

And there the kite stayed, and wouldn't move. The toys laughed at it. They pulled its tail. They unwound its string and got it all muddled.

The kite was very upset. "Don't do that," it said. "I may want that string some day."

"Pooh! What for?" cried the teddy bear. "What do kites do? Nothing, so far as I can see! Except just lie in the cupboard and get lazier and lazier." And the bad bear tangled the strings up even more.

The kite was very unhappy about it, for it had no arms or legs to undo the knots. But the little white ostrich out of the Noah's Ark was very kind. She came up to undo the tangle. And very soon the kite and the ostrich made friends.

"Where's the other ostrich?" asked the kite. "I thought there were two of every animal and bird in the ark."

"Well, there *were* two ostriches," said the little white ostrich, "but the other one got trodden on and broken. So now there is only me. And I am often lonely because I am by myself. The other animals are in pairs."

"Don't be lonely," said the kite. "Come and talk to me when you feel sad."

So after that the ostrich and the kite often talked together, though everyone else laughed at them.

"What you can see in that silly, quiet kite I really can't imagine!" said the teddy bear to the ostrich.

"And what the kite can see in that stupid little wooden ostrich puzzles *me*!" said the red-haired doll, tossing her thick ponytail.

Now one day, the wind got up out-of-doors and roared away into the sky, blowing the clouds along and twisting the chimney smoke like ribbon. And into the playroom ran John and Lucy, to whom all the toys belonged.

"Where's our kite? Where's our kite?" John cried. "It's just the day for a kite! Kite, where are you?"

He pulled the kite out of the cupboard and shook its tail. "Come along!" he cried. "It's just the day for a fine kite like you!"

"Oh, good, John. You've found the kite," said Lucy. "Let's take all the toys into the garden so they can watch."

So they picked up the toys, little white ostrich and all, and took them into the garden. The toys were most surprised. What was all this fuss about the kite? Why was this windy day just the day for it? They simply couldn't imagine!

The children set the toys down on the grass.
John began to unwind a little of the string that was
tied to the kite. He shook out the lovely long tail.

The wind caught hold of the kite and pulled at it
in delight. John threw it up into the air. At once it
rose high, and higher still as John let out more and
more string. It quivered and shook like a live
thing. Its lovely tail swung below it, twisting and
shaking. It was marvellous!

"Oh, Lucy! Doesn't the kite fly beautifully?"
cried John, pleased. "It's the best kite in the
world. Oh, look it's pulling so hard at my hand
that it feels like a horse wanting to gallop away!"

"Well, hold on tight," said Lucy. "It would be
dreadful if you let go and it flew away by itself!
Hold on tight!"

All the toys watched in amazement. Could this
really be the poor quiet kite they had so often

laughed at? The kite that had no legs and couldn't play with them? The kite whom they had teased and tangled? They couldn't believe it! It was flying higher and higher in the air, sometimes dipping down in great circles, sometimes flapping its tail in glee. It was lovely to watch.

"Would you believe that the quiet old kite could fly like that?" said the red-haired doll.

"*I* couldn't fly up in the air," said the teddy.

"It's much, much cleverer than we are," said the train.

The little white ostrich was proud of her fine friend. She watched out of her black eyes and wondered if the kite would bump into the big white clouds that raced along so fast.

At last the wind dropped and the kite swooped down. It lay on the grass quite quiet. John and Lucy heard their mother calling.

"Come on—that's Mother," said John. "She has some biscuits for us!" And they both raced indoors.

Soon the wind began to blow again and the kite lifted itself a little from the grass. "Ostrich," it called, "climb on to my tail! I'll give you a fly! You are a nice little bird and you ought to try how lovely it is to fly through the air!"

"Ostriches don't fly. They only run!" called the teddy bear, jealously. He would so very much have loved to climb on to the end of the kite's tail himself.

"*This* ostrich is going to fly!" said the little white ostrich, and she settled herself on the very end of the kite's tail. There came a great gust of wind and the kite rose up joyously. It flew up into the air, dragging its long tail behind it. And on the end flew the little white ostrich half delighted, half frightened, but enjoying herself thoroughly.

"The kite will fly away and John and Lucy will be cross," said the teddy. But this time Lucy had been careful. She had tied the end of the kite's string to a post. So when the kite rose very high it had to stay there. The string was tied fast to the post and the kite couldn't get away.

Soon John and Lucy came out with their biscuits. "Look!" cried Lucy. "The kite is flying itself. Isn't it clever!"

When he pulled down the kite to put it away, John had such a surprise. He called to Lucy. "Lucy! Look! The little white ostrich has been for a fly on the tail of the kite! Isn't that odd?"

When the kite was put away in the toy cupboard that night, the toys came up to it. They felt ashamed.

"Kite, you were marvellous today," said the red-haired doll.

"Kite, I'm sorry I tangled your string," said the bear. "I didn't know how important your string was to you."

"It's quite all right," said the kite generously. "I know I'm quiet and dull when I'm lying here doing nothing, but I'm a different fellow, I can tell you, when I'm up in the air!"

"Give the others a ride on your tail next time," said the little white ostrich, who was pleased to find that the toys were being nice to her friend.

"I will!" said the kite. And it'll keep its word, no doubt about that. I'd love to see the red-haired doll swinging on the end of its tail, wouldn't you?